The Other Place
A Medieval Murder Mystery play about the founding of Cambridge University

Kevin Mahoney

Punked Books

Published in 2017 by Punked Books
An Authortrek imprint
www.authortrek.com/punked-books

Cover image ©istockphoto.com/ Mercy_C_M_H

ISBN 978-1-908375-32-2

A catalogue record for this book is available from the British Library.

Characters

Erik Danby

Erika Danby

Freydis Danby (mother of Erik and Erika)

Alice de Blois

Roger de Blois

Caradoc

Henry le Coq

Robert de Crepon

William de Blois

Laurence Kepeharm

Philip Molendinarius (aka Philip the Miller)

Mathilda

Guy Deschamps

Rosie

Richard Woodnutt

Mr Killingback

Mrs Casburn

Mr Badcock

Mr Doggett

ACT 1
SCENE 1

We begin with a shadow play dramatization of the hanging of two men.
Erik Danby narrates off stage.

ERIK: I hated the men that I hung so much that I didn't care whether they'd killed her or not. I was just so full of rage that somebody had to die. Besides, they were always looking down on me, but now they were doing so from a somewhat less privileged vantage point than they had done so previously!

There is a shadow play dramatization of a group of men packing bags and leaving town, carrying bindles on a pole like Dick Whittington, as Erik Danby continues his narration.

ERIK: I watched with glee as the rats scurried away from the ship. I thanked God that the likes of them would never disgrace the good city of Oxford again. And yet my life was not always so full of pain and suffering.

SCENE 2

The shadow play screen is moved away to reveal a woman screaming in pain while sitting on a birthing stool in a rich medieval home. The expectant mother is Alice de Blois. A visual effect provides the illusion of an open fire and smoke. Freydis Danby is attending to the expectant mother.
We also see the exterior of the home (trees and grass) where the young twins Erik and Erika Danby are playing.

ERIK: Tag, you're it!

Erika easily catches up with Erik and tags him.

ERIKA: You're it!

Erika runs away to stop Erik from tagging her. Erik runs after her, and Erika zigzags this way and that. A surly young boy (Roger de Blois) runs by and trips up Erik just as he is about to tag Erika.

ERIK: Oy! What are you playing at?

Erik pushes back at Roger, and their conflict soon develops into a full-blown fight. At one point Erik stands aside from the affray, but Erika pushes him back into it.

ERIK: Who the hell do you think you are, pushing me around like this? I'm of Danish stock, so you'd better watch out!

ROGER: You're really a Wicing? I think that you're more of a lily livered Saxon!

ERIK: Who are you? I've never seen you before.

ROGER: I'm Roger de Blois, and I'm descended from real Northmen. This is my land, not for scum like you. I'm a scholar. I wouldn't usually have anything to do with peasants like you, but beating you is fun. What are you doing on my land, you wretch?

5

ERIK: My mother's doing a birthing.

ROGER: If it were up to my father, that witch would never be allowed near my mother.

ERIK: Who are you calling a witch?

ROGER: Your mother's a witch, Wicing!

Meanwhile, Freydis has been getting more and more anxious about the state of the expectant mother. She goes to the door of the lying in room and shouts out to her children. Despite her evident concern, her voice is not too anxious, so as not to worry the mother.

FREYDIS: Erik! Erika! I need little hands.

ROGER: Shall I fetch my father and the surgeon?

FREYDIS: Don't worry little one, your mother's in safe hands.

Erika and Erik run into the lying in room.

FREYDIS: Erika, the baby's head is in the wrong position. I need you to move it.

ERIKA: Okay mum.

Erika rolls up her sleeves and begins to work on the expectant mother.

ALICE: Is everything all right?

FREYDIS: Don't worry dear, my daughter has excellent hands, and has helped deliver many hundreds of little babes. My son has also helped in the birth of many a lamb.

To Erik.

FREYDIS: Don't stand there gawping! Get the crane's foot! And open all the cupboards!

Freydis undoes the plaits in Alice's hair.

ALICE: Don't you have an incantation that you can... cant? I'm in agony here! I thought Roger was bad, but this is torture!

FREYDIS: Don't you worry my dear; we've opened all the cupboards and doors, so your babe will soon run free. And I have an incantation that always works. Ab irato, ab inconvenienti, ab incunabulis, ab initio, ab intra, ab origine, absit omen, a capite ad calcem, ad augusta per angusta, alea iacta est, alma mater, ante mortem, a pedibus usque ad caput...

ERIKA: Auribus teneo lupum!

Erika holds aloft a wailing newborn. Erik skulks off outside to play, but is jumped upon and beaten by Roger who then runs away. Erik starts to cry. Caradoc, an Augustine monk, stops by.

CARADOC: What's happened here Erik?

ERIK: Roger de Blois hit me! Look, there's blood all over my leg.

CARADOC: Oh dear, that doesn't look good. Perhaps his parents should put up a "Cave Canem" sign.

ERIK: Cave canem?

CARADOC: Latin for "Beware of the Dog". All these scholars are dogs, in my opinion, but they'll be surprised one day when one of the pups of the town bite back. Come, let's tend to your wounds in the mighty flowing waters of Isis.

ERIK: You'll not convert me to your religious ways there!

CARADOC: Don't worry Erik, I've no desire to baptise a heathen, although I've seen many soul like you lost in Isis. Come now, or do you want to run home for mummy to attend your wounds?

7

SCENE 3

Caradoc is rolling a barrel of ale into Freydis's alehouse, the Bear Inn, whistling as he goes.

CARADOC: Put out the ale-wand missus, for I have a barrel of the finest from St. Fridewide's here.

FREYDIS: Will you stay to sup a pint Caradoc?

CARADOC: Well, you know what I always say, Corripe Cervisiam!

FREYDIS: Seize the beer indeed! Erik and Erika! Bring out the stools!

We hear Erika's voice offstage.

ERIKA: Birthing, drinking or pooping?

FREYDIS: Drinking!

Caradoc drinks the ale that Freydis has poured for him.

CARADOC: Very satisfying. Not as pleasant as your own sweet ale Freydis, but altogether not bad.

FREYDIS: I'm not sure that you'll ever taste my sweet ale again...

Caradoc grabs her by the waist.

CARADOC: Tell me that it ain't so!

Freydis disentangles herself. The now adult Erik sullenly puts out stools.

FREYDIS: ...due to all the babes that are being born, as I was about to say.

CARADOC: Could we not add to their number Freydis?

FREYDIS: You ought to be ashamed of yourself Caradoc, talking that way, with you being a married man.

CARADOC: Married?

FREYDIS: Yea, married to God. We all know how faithful you are to your betrothed.

Caradoc puts his hands together in mock prayer.

FREYDIS: 'Sides, you could never handle a woman of the world like me.

CARADOC: I could give it a try. I'm not afraid of you, Freydis.

FREYDIS: I'm sure you could "give it a try" for all of five seconds Caradoc. Besides, if I'm put in the family way, then who would look after all the babes of the lusty clerks of this town?

CARADOC: Don't talk to me about clerks, snooty bastards. I know more about what's in the Good Book then any of those so-called "theologians".

FREYDIS: You ought to be the town cryer: you're always saying the same thing.

CARADOC: Don't defend the clerks and scholars. You know they look down on all of us. Especially when they're in the sack!

FREYDIS: You jealous of them Caradoc? You with your teeny weeney peeney?

CARADOC: I'm serious now. You should see the way that Henry le Coq, Robert de Crepon and their ilk stare at Erika. You can almost see the semen drooling out of their mouths.

FREYDIS: And what do you know of semen Caradoc? I've seen you hanging around by the Grandpont... You should take one of them young clerks as one of your fancies - then you can truly bugger them

9

as you desire.

CARADOC: I'd never do a thing like that! You know what the Bible says: "qui dormierit cum masculo coitu femineo uterque operati sunt nefas morte moriantur sit sanguis eorum super eos."

FREYDIS: "If a man also lie with mankind, as he lieth with a woman, both of them have committed an abomination: they shall surely be put to death; their blood shall be upon them" blah de blah, yawn. Yet all you monks do it.

CARADOC: You know it's only you Freydis that makes my life so hard and my dreams so wet...

FREYDIS: It's only the ale that ails you at night, that's what makes your peeney drip.

CARADOC: True enough! There's strength in this here bile. What about you Erik? What's wrong?

ERIK: Nothing.

CARADOC: There must be something wrong. You look as if a cat had sucked your cock instead of a pussy. Girl trouble? Pull up a pew.

ERIK: It's Erika...

CARADOC: That's a new one. What happened to Mathilda? Did you till her?

ERIK: Erika's my sister!

CARADOC: You want to keep it in the family way? Mmmmmmm...

ERIK: I think Roger de Blois is courting her. I caught them giggling last night.

The inn is beginning to fill up. Two young clerks, Henry le Coq and Robert de Crepon are awkwardly standing around. Erika addresses

10

them.

ERIKA: What's wrong with you two? Looks like you've never been in an inn before. I've warmed up a couple of seats for you in the corner.

HENRY: Th-th-thank you.

CARADOC: It's them two you want to look out for, as I told your mother earlier - Henry le Coq and Robert de Crepon.

ERIK: Those two! I've never met less of a cock than him and his cretin. They wouldn't know what to do with her if she fell into their laps and started licking their balls!

CARADOC: Oh, I don't know. On their own they'd be fine, but the two of them? They might get bold one day. They both look as though they've got blades in their pockets...

ERIK: They've just got hard-ons. We all get them. Even a man of a cloth like you, I daresay. It's just Roger de Blois... Ah! I'd like to smash his face in, the way he looks at her.

CARADOC: You've never got on with him have you? Especially not when you were kids. I remember all too well you coming to cry to me after all the beatings he gave you. Although Roger's much better than his "holier than thou" father. I can see what your sister sees in him, nice handsome lad like that.

ERIK: If it were anyone but him!

CARADOC: Do I detect a hint of jealousy here? Erika always took Roger's side when you were kids. That must have been galling, to be constantly betrayed and teased by your own twin?

ERIK: That's nothing to do with it! I've always known that he's got evil in place of a heart.

CARADOC: Just because he used to pinch and punch you when you were a lad?

11

ERIK: He'll have his way with her and then she'll be ruined!

CARADOC: Oh, come on! Nobody is pure in this town, not even me, and certainly not God above. Just let him have her. Let him have her.

ERIK: What?

CARADOC: I'll regale you with a little pearl of wisdom from the Bible. You ever heard the story of Amnon and Tamar?

ERIK: No.

CARADOC: I'll forgive you; it's not one they read out from the pulpit every Sunday. (Or any Sunday for that matter.) Amnon, not Solomon, was the eldest son of King David. Well, one day, he had the hots for a little totty called Tamar. So he pretended to be ill one day, and sent a message to Tamar to cook him some "meat", as this would make him feel better. Having some affection for him, Tamar agreed. However, when Tamar arrived, he ravished her...

ERIK: He raped her?

CARADOC: Don't be surprised, there's lots of rape and pillage in the Bible. Anyway, when Amnon had had his way with Tamar, he felt disgusted by her, sent her on her way, and never had anything to do with her again. That what makes me think that it's a true story. Haven't you ever lusted after a whore, and then be disgusted with her after you'd finished?

ERIK: No.

CARADOC: You know your problem, you idolise women too much, her especially. You should just take her for yourself and have done with it. Show her who the man is.

ERIK: What? She's my sister!

CARADOC: That didn't stop Amnon, son of David. Tamar was his half-sister, after all. No, you just have your way with Erika, get it out of your system with your sister, and then you'll be fine. Since she's your twin, it'll just be like masturbating I expect.

ERIK: You disgust me sometimes; call yourself a man of the cloth. You're no better than the clerks.

CARADOC: Speaking of which...

Caradoc draws attention to the fact that Henry le Coq has just tried to kiss Erika when she brought he and Robert ale.

ERIK: Little bastards!

ROGER: Get your hands off her, you twats!

Roger seizes Robert and Henry. Erik in turn pushes Roger aside.

ERIK: Leave them to me. She's my sister!

Roger takes affront at this and Erik and Roger begin to scuffle. Henry and Robert quietly escape. Erik punches Roger. Erika jumps in between them and gives Erik a good slap.

ERIKA: I can take care of myself. I don't need either of you two watching my back.

William de Blois, Roger's father, enters with Laurence Kepeharm.

WILLIAM: I thought I'd find you here in this den of iniquity. I don't know what's up with you. First, I find you carousing at the fair, and then I find you in this dump. You should be at home with your wife.

ROGER: Thank you father.

Erika slaps Roger. The crowd in the tavern roar and cheer.

ERIKA: Since when were you married?

WILLIAM: Since All Souls', you little whore.

Erik balls up his fists and rushes at William, but Laurence restrains him. In the process, William backs away from Erik so much that he bumps into Freydis, and has to grab a hold of her to prevent himself from falling.

WILLIAM: That's right Laurence Kepeharm, keep me from harm.

FREYDIS: Don't you have any milk you need to sour in your cloister?

WILLIAM: If I had my way, witches like you madam would be relieved of your genitals, hung, disembowelled, beheaded and your limbs torn from your body. Indeed, I have written to the King suggesting such a punishment for murder. And whores like your daughter would be cleaned off the street. This should be a town of scholars, not scum!

CARADOC: I thought that you were in dispute with the King. Is this your way of cuddling up to him? Be careful, or you may well end up being hung, drawn and quartered yourself.

WILLIAM: While the King and the Church may well violently disagree over the choice of the next Archbishop, there are many things on which we see eye to eye, such as the due punishment for wanton murder.

CARADOC: I wouldn't be so sure of that. His father killed Becket, and King John's an irascible...

FREYDIS: Your wife was already dead when I came to deliver you thirteenth child. I had to cut her open, to save your child! But you're right. There will come a day when men like you will usurp your will upon "old hags" like me with impunity. I'm just glad that I won't be here to see it. Although you'll be shaking in your grave seven hundred years from now when there'll be women scholars in this town.

WILLIAM: See how she prophesizes the future! I've never seen or heard such a godless prophet before. Women scholars? Pah! Surgery is

14

a man's job, you know that. Just as midwifery is supposed to be a woman's job. Before she died, my wife told me of what role your son plays at the births.

FREYDIS: Alice could never tell the twins apart. Besides, you wouldn't have been born if it were not for the likes of me. Although you had thirteen kids, you didn't really know your way around your wife's body - she certainly told me that afore she died! Now, good day to you, Sir.

LAURENCE: That's enough gents, be on your way now.

Laurence gestures that both William and Roger should leave.

WILLIAM: That's right Kepeharm, keep me from harm, as you always do.

William and Roger exit. Erika quietly follows them soon after, although Erik notices and follows her in turn.

LAURENCE: I'd like to punch that bastard in the face.

CARADOC: But then you'd probably have to arrest yourself, Sheriff.

LAURENCE: I'm not the sheriff anyone. Haven't been so for a year or so.

CARADOC: So who's the sheriff now then?

LAURENCE: Philip Molendinarius.

CARADOC: Philip the Miller? I'm trembling already!

SCENE 4

Erik chases after Erika on Oxford High Street, but a woman blocks his way.

ERIK: Mathilda! I didn't see you there.

MATHILDA: Chasing after your sister as usual I see. If only you paid me the same attention, your betrothed!

ERIK: Sorry Mathilda, this isn't a great time.

MATHILDA: It's never a great time, is it? I'm sure your mother's happy running the inn on her own while you two are gallivanting about.

ERIK: We've just found out from Roger's own mouth that he's married.

MATHILDA: Interesting, but so what? Isn't this what you wanted? Some excuse for Roger to dump Erika?

ERIK: But she's going to be devastated! I think she really loved him. I knew he was going to do this to her. I've known all along how much of an arrogant bastard he is, now everyone else can finally see it.

MATHILDA: Well, now that that is over, how about us?

ERIK: What do you mean, how about us?

Mathilda gives him a slap.

MATHILDA: In case you've forgotten, I'm pregnant. You will do the right thing by me, even if I have to kill you to do it.

ERIK: We're already married in the eyes of God.

MATHILDA: It's not the eyes of God that bother me; it's everybody else's eyes.

Erik bends down on one knee.

ERIK: If it will stop you nagging, Mathilda would you do me the great honour...

Mathilda pulls him up to his feet.

MATHILDA: Not here. I don't want everyone to see.

ERIK: But I thought that was the whole point.

MATHILDA: I don't want to do it here in front of everyone's Saturday night out.

ERIK: That didn't seem to bother you when we first did it. Look, why don't we just go back to the inn and do it there? I'm sure the lads wouldn't want to miss out.

MATHILDA: But I want it to be romantic, in the countryside...

ERIK: Okay, well then we can head out to Broken Hays now if you like.

MATHILDA: No, not now. I don't want to go to the country at night, it'll scare me. Besides "Broken Hays" sounds too much like "broken vows" and I've had enough of those from you already.

ERIK: It's not necessary to get married in a church.

MATHILDA: Yuck! I wouldn't want to get married in front of one of them creepy scholars. I've rather vomit. In fact, I think I may be about to... Damned morning sickness, and it's bloody evening!

ERIK: It's not too late for you to change your mind. My mother can take care of the baby for you.

MATHILDA: I'm not worried about that. Your mother's talked me through it already. I'll be prepared when the time comes.

17

ERIK: No, I meant that...

MATHILDA: Don't you worry; your mother's going to take me out to one of her birthings. Nothing like seeing the real thing to set your mind at ease.

ERIK: I wouldn't be too sure of that.

MATHILDA: Well, what would you know? You're a man. But I trust your mother. I'll be safe in her hands. In fact, I'm quite looking forward to it. It's been ages since our Rosie was born, and I was just a kid then, so I can't really remember it. Maybe I'll even get to lend a hand... Oh, I do love babies.

ERIK: So I've discovered. But are you sure? You know it's a big risk. Maybe a third of pregnant mothers die... Are you sure you want to go through that?

MATHILDA: You're a barrel of laughs. Besides, hardly any of your mother's mothers die. Why do you think I picked you? I could hardly be in safer hands.

ERIK: And there was me thinking that you just liked me for my good looks.

MATHILDA: Oh no, I assure you there's a plan in which you'll make me happily ever after.

ERIK: In the meantime, do you mind if I run out after my sister before she does something stupid?

MATHILDA: She'll be fine, don't you worry. Erika can always look after herself, as I'm sure she's told you many a time.

ERIK: Well, I'd like to be sure, just in case.

Erik heads up the street in the same direction as Erika.

MATHILDA: If only you cared for me as much. Well, I guess twins will be twins. Speaking of twins... Maybe they run in the family! I hope I haven't bitten off more than I can chew.

SCENE 5

Erik finally manages to catch up to Erika.

ERIKA: Leave me alone. I don't want to talk about it.

ERIK: I'm sorry Erika, but I knew he'd do this to you. I did try to warn you.

ERIKA: This is your fault. You've always been trying to push him away. All because you've got this thing about scholars.

ERIK: Well, if he hadn't given me a bloody nose the first day I met him, that might have helped. Besides, the scholars live in another world - they're not like us. His father would never have let you marry him. Even if his father weren't a pompous ass, he would never have let you marry him. You know their sort don't - can't marry our sort.

ERIKA: Marriage! Babies, mother-in-laws et cetera. That's not what I wanted from him.

ERIK: Well, his mother's dead, for a start. You know that - you were there when she died.

ERIKA: I know that Erik! I was speaking generally.

ERIK: So what did you want from him, money? Wait - did he pay you? The little bastard!

ERIKA: No, it was never like that, despite what his father thinks. No, it was love. That's all I ever wanted, and he gave it to me in bucket loads.

ERIK: I bet he did, while you were in bed.

ERIKA: Well, what do you know about love?

ERIK: I love you, and mother loves you. I'll always be here to protect you.

ERIKA: I don't need your protection. I can look after myself. And I don't need your jealousy, because that's what it is, not love!

ERIK: I can't help the way I feel about you Erika - I never have. We've always been so alike. I still feel as if we're the same person.

ERIKA: Oh, grow up Erik! It's not like we're completely identical. If we were, you'd have tits and a pussy, which I'm sure you'd love.

ERIK: Why are you being like this Erika? We used to be so close before Roger de Blois came along.

ERIKA: When mummy used to dress us up in the same sackcloth, you mean? Look, I just want to be my own person. The twin thing - that was fun when we were young, but we're grown-up now. And I just want to do my own thing, be my own person, without my halfwit brother hanging around while I track down Roger.

ERIK: You're not still after him, are you? After what he's done to you?

ERIKA: So what if I am? I still love him, and he loves me.

ERIK: But you'd be living in sin!

ERIKA: You sound like one of them scholars! Living in sin, hah! I'll be more of a wife to him that any snobby wretch his father got to marry him.

ERIK: But you don't have to do this. Find someone else.

ERIKA: What, are you worried that he's going to break my poor heart?

ERIK: He already has, hasn't he?

ERIKA: Well, as you say, he was always going to marry someone else. That's how things work. Just happened a little sooner than I expected.

ERIK: And how would you feel if you had to attend one of the birthings?

ERIKA: Rather them than me, that's what I say. I've seen enough puking babies to last me a lifetime, thanks to dear mother. I don't want to do any more of that birthing crap.

ERIK: But mother's depending on you to carry on the line...

ERIKA: What? Or else her "special" knowledge is just going to disappear? Well, I'm sorry to disappoint you, but babies are going to continue being born, whether or not I take part in it. That's nature.

ERIK: But she knows so much. You know other midwives aren't so smart. Alice de Blois and their ilk are just the rare exceptions.

ERIKA: You know who's smart? I'll tell you who's smart. Roger's got more intellect than a dozen of your friends. He's been places you've never heard of, and knows things you'll never learn. I have an inkling, 'cos he taught me how to read. There's marvellous worlds in those books.

ERIK: Who's sounding like a scholar now? And how did his father ever let you get hold of a book?

ERIKA: Just some of the textbooks he had when he was younger, full of the most marvellous myths and heroes. I'd loved to be one of those epic heroines.

ERIK: They were always being raped, so Caradoc tells me.

ERIKA: So you know something of them too? But more than that, Roger treats me as an equal. We have our own special jokes - mostly involving you. Don't look so sour! I'm only joking. I suppose you'd want me to marry that pig-headed John Pady. Nothing good will come of him.

22

ERIK: John's a good lad. He has some wealth. He'd look after you very well.

ERIKA: But he's as dull as hell. He's got nothing of the thrill that I get from being with Roger.

ERIK: But you can't keep with Roger. He doesn't love you.

ERIKA: He does! I know he does.

ERIK: If he loves you so much, then why didn't he tell you about the marriage?

ERIKA: 'Cos he knows that I don't care about that kind of thing. We're soulmates, he and I, and nothing will ever come between us.

ERIK: You're deluding yourself.

ERIKA: Oh, what do you know about women? You think because you got Mathilda up the duff, and because you jealousy guard mummy's crane foot that you know anything about women? Just because mummy let you hear the cries of labour, and you've seen the odd pussy or two, that you think you know about women? Thanks to mummy's twisted parenting skills, you have a really mucked up worldview. Most midwives have more common sense - they don't bring their kids along to every birth. No wonder you know nothing about romance. Roger knows more than you'll ever do. He's a real man of the world, unlike you.

ERIK: But if you keep with Roger, it'll be exactly like what his father says.

ERIKA: What do you mean?

ERIK: Well his father's always calling you a whore...

ERIKA: Don't you judge me. Never judge me. You don't possess me. I do not belong to you. God help Mathilda! And don't you dare follow me!

ERIK: Where are you going? We're needed back at the inn. Mum will be going mental.

Henry le Coq and Robert de Crepon are staggering up the High Street, squabbling over a flask of ale. Erika snatches it off them and starts drinking from it as she hurries along.

ERIKA: I'm going to hang out with all the lads on Gropecunt lane, like a real whore. Don't you dare follow me, or I'll smash out your brains with this flask. Don't think I won't do it - as mum always says, I'm a Dane!

ERIK: But that road leads to Roger's house! Christ! Well, on your own head be it. Don't say I didn't warn you.

ACT 2
SCENE 1

The next morning, Erik walks into the bear inn. He's evidently had a rough night. After a little, Freydis also comes in, searching frantically for something. Caradoc is snoozing on a table, and disturbed by Freydis' searching, eventually yawns and groans.

CARADOC: What? Have I missed Matins again? The Prior will be pissed.

FREYDIS: I think it's you who are pissed, dear friend.

CARADOC: Well, as I always say, uxor formosa et vinum sunt dulcia venena!

FREYDIS: Indeed. Erik, have you seen my blade? Joan Berford is nine days' over, and I think that I'll have need of it.

ERIK: No, I've not seen it.

CARADOC: What's the matter with you boy? It looks like you have a malady.

ERIK: It feels as though my stomach has seven stones in it this morning.

FREYDIS: Aw! Wine mars beauty and destroys the freshness of youth.

CARADOC: Couldn't have said it better myself!

ERIK: I drank nothing but two beakers of ale last night, along with some bread and honey. Then I wake up in the middle of the night with this stabbing pain in my stomach.

CARADOC: Where is Erika? Is she suffering from the same alement? Ha ha. You know, I've often heard it said that twins feel the same even from afar.

FREYDIS: Well then, Erik and Erika well may feel a boot up the bum sometime soon! Where is that girl? What happened to you both last night? You left me here on my own while Joan's so late?

ERIK: I thought Mathilda would be helping you out from now on. That's what she told me last night.

FREYDIS: I don't want to give her a fright by cutting Joan in front of her, if it comes to that.

CARADOC: Do you need me on hand to perform the baptism rites?

FREYDIS: I can do that myself. Besides, as you well know, there are no men at the lying in.

CARADOC: You sure you don't want Nicholas de Farnham or any of his scholars handy?

FREYDIS: I'm sure de Farnham wouldn't deign to come to a townswoman like Joan. And the reason why Joan got in this state in the first place is due to a scholar dipping his blade into her. No, I have no need of such a callow youth. Speaking of callow youths, where did you get to last night Erik? Courting Mathilda I presume?

ERIK: I ran out after Erika. You know that she's still determined to keep with Roger, even though he's married?

FREYDIS: I thought as much.

ERIK: And it doesn't bother you? He'll ruin her!

FREYDIS: You sound like William de Blois! What, have you become a scholar now? All the while you complain about their snobbishness, but you're just as snooty as they are.

ERIK: She's my twin!

FREYDIS: She stopped being your twin a long time ago.

26

CARADOC: About when she developed some tits and ass, if I remember rightly. Sorry - just trying to help.

ERIK: He'll shame her!

FREYDIS: Erika learnt enough from me about how to prevent babes. She's well practised at it. And if she did get in the family way, then I'm on hand to help her. She knows enough about birthings to help herself, I shouldn't wonder.

ERIK: You mean she and Erik have been at it all this time? And you let her? Just you wait till I get my hands on her, I'll kill her!

CARADOC: Quia peccavi nimis cogitatione, verbo et opere: mea culpa, mea culpa, mea maxima culpa.

FREYDIS: You'll do no such thing! Heavens! How many birthings did I take you to when you were young where the woman was out of wedlock?

ERIK: There were so many that I can hardly remember.

FREYDIS: Exactly. All of them good decent women, most of them taken by preachy clerks who couldn't keep their hose in their hose.

ERIK: Erika's heading that way too, thanks to you. She said she was going to Gropecunt lane.

FREYDIS: Well, I'm sure she was joking. You know what she's like.

Laurence runs into the inn, followed by a panting Philip the Miller.

LAURENCE: We've found Erika!

FREYDIS: Good, good.

There is a pause as Laurence and Philip look awkwardly at each other.

27

FREYDIS: Well, what's keeping her? You're not keeping her in the keep are you?

PHILIP: She's in a ditch on Alfred Street.

FREYDIS: What? You couldn't carry her between you, two big strong men like you? Well, what state is she in?

LAURENCE: She's dead.

ERIK: What? You're having a laugh.

PHILIP: We think she's been murdered.

FREYDIS: Think? Think? The men of this town are so good at thinking.

CARADOC: And not so good at drinking. Sorry - just trying to lighten the mood.

ERIK: Shut it, monkface!

Freydis frantically continues her searching.

LAURENCE: What are you doing?

FREYDIS: Searching for my blade. I'm going to need it!

ERIK: Joan can wait! She's been waiting long enough. Another few days isn't going to... Going to...

Erik abruptly heads to the door, but Laurence stops him.

LAURENCE: Where do you think you're off to?

ERIK: I've got to see her... I've got to see what Roger's done to her.

LAURENCE: I don't think you want to do that, I really don't.

FREYDIS: Let him go! He's seen enough blood and guts in his time, thanks to me.

LAURENCE: Alright, alright. But no shouting off about Roger, you hear me? We don't know for sure who's done this.

FREYDIS: Then you'd better find out quickly, hadn't you? Before this town erupts with more blood and guts.

Erik, Freydis, Laurence, Philip and Caradoc are standing in Alfred Street, staring at the bloody corpse.

CARADOC: Per istam sanctan unctionem et suam piissimam misErikordiam...

FREYDIS: Isn't it a bit too bloody late for that?

CARADOC: Sorry, I thought that I... I just had to say something.

FREYDIS: You usually do.

Freydis gathers Erik and Caradoc into a hug and leads them aside for a moment.

PHILIP: I never expected this. Knobbing with the King, and chucking a few drunks in the keep - that's what you said.

LAURENCE: There's more to this job than lining your purse, miller.

PHILIP: Well, what do we do now? Have you ever seen anything like this?

LAURENCE: Nothing since the days I did my own butchering at the farm. Although I did hear a few years ago about some women that had been found in Reading, who had been skinned to the bone.

PHILIP: What have they done to her?

LAURENCE: What does it look like?

PHILIP: I dunno. The only guts I've ever seen were hung up to dry in the marketplace.

LAURENCE: I'm no expert, but it looks like her intestines have been moved.

PHILIP: And her a midwife... Jesus Christ! Who would know how to do a thing like that?

LAURENCE: Nicholas de Farnham...

PHILIP: You think a scholar did it? The townsmen will never stand for that.

LAURENCE: He or one of his scholars. Any butcher or barber would know. So, quite a few people. Then there's her mother and her brother... They'd know how to do this.

ERIK: I heard that! What, you think I'd kill my own sister! My twin!

CARADOC: Well, you did say you could kill her earlier, back at the inn.

ERIK: But I didn't mean it! Why would I kill my own bloody sister?

LAURENCE: Because you didn't like who she was consorting with, and wanted to preserve her - your honour perhaps?

FREYDIS: Don't be so bloody stupid, Laurence. It's quite clear that whoever did this has a hatred of women. You see how her womb has been removed.

LAURENCE: Her womb? That puts a different complexion on things. (*Pause*). You seem unusually calm madam.

FREYDIS: I've seen a few bloody bodies before in my line of work, as you well know.

ERIK: Removed the womb? It must have been Roger, I'm telling you. She was talking about having babies. He must have killed her and the child. I'm going to bloody kill him! I'll kill him!

Some men in armour arrive and look questioningly at Philip.

LAURENCE: And not before time! Bang him in irons!

31

The soldiers are still looking at Philip.

PHILIP: Very well, you two take him away.

Two of the soldiers take Erik away, kicking and screaming.

ERIK: I'll kill him! I'll bloody kill him!

LAURENCE: Gag him too, for Christ's sake.

FREYDIS: He hasn't done anything Laurence! He's a hotheaded lout, but he'd never kill his own sister!

LAURENCE: That's as may be. What I want to avoid is him starting a riot. Don't just stand there; get a bloody cart to take the body away!

Some of the soldiers run off to get a cart.

LAURENCE: Now who lives in this house here?

CARADOC: You don't think whoever killed her would be stupid enough to leave her on their own doorstep, do you?

LAURENCE: Stranger things have happened. If she wasn't killed here, then she can't have been killed far away. Somebody would have seen the killer moving the body, even if it was in the early hours of the morning.

The soldiers arrive with the cart and load the body onto it. As they do so, a blade drops from Erika's hand.

PHILIP: What was that?

LAURENCE: The murder weapon I bet. Take it back to the castle too.

FREYDIS: That's my blade!

PHILIP: What?

FREYDIS: It's the knife I use to cut women open when they're dying. To save the baby.

CARADOC: You mean a Caesarean operation?

FREYDIS: Of course, yes.

LAURENCE: You'd best go to the castle too.

Some of the soldiers grab Freydis by the arms.

LAURENCE: I'm sure that's not necessary, let her go.

PHILIP: Take her to my office, and provide her with any comfort she needs.

LAURENCE: And take the body back to the castle quickly. With any luck we can do this quietly before any more townsfolk wake.

Philip gestures to the soldiers to take the body away. Freydis takes the lead as they walk away.

FREYDIS: If only I could unsee this sight!

LAURENCE: Have some men search this house.

Philip gestures that they do so.

PHILIP: What do you think they'll find?

LAURENCE: Some blood, hopefully.

Henry le Coq pops his head out of one of the house's windows.

HENRY: What's going on down there? Some of us are trying to b-b-bloody sleep!

Robert de Crepon also sticks his head out of the window.

ROBERT: Yeah, go to hell... Sorry, I didn't see you there. (*To Henry*). You didn't tell me there were bloody soldiers!

Robert and Henry go back inside, but we can still hear them bickering with each other.

CARADOC: Well, that's an unexpected piece of luck!

LAURENCE: What are you standing there for, you gormless lumps! Get them!

The soldiers pile on into the house and drag out Henry and Robert kicking and screaming. They also take away another clerk from the house, Guy Deschamps.

SCENE 3

Erik is in the dungeon of Oxford castle, holding onto the bars. Laurence, Philip, Caradoc walk in, followed by the soldiers restraining Henry, Robert and Guy.

ERIK: Let me... What the hell are they doing here?

CARADOC: Would you believe it? They live in the house next to where your sister was found.

ERIK: What? I'll bloody kill them!

LAURENCE: I think that's quite enough from you, Caradoc. It's time you finally got back to your own cell.

GUY: What the hell's going on? What are we doing here?

PHILIP: As if you didn't know!

ERIK: I'll kill you for what you did to my sister!

HENRY: I'm s-s-sorry. It was just a p-p-peck on the cheek.

ERIK: I'll kill you!

ROBERT: Don't put us in there with him, he'll kill us!

PHILIP: That's probably as much as you deserve!

LAURENCE: I think the scholars are talking sense... for a change. Put them in the other cell.

PHILIP: Very well.

The scholars are locked in the adjacent cell to Erik.

LAURENCE: And let us repair to your office. This din is doing my head in.

SCENE 4

Freydis is sitting at a desk in Philip's office. Laurence and Philip enter.

FREYDIS: You've kept me waiting long enough!

LAURENCE: Now then madam, how is it that your blade ended up in your dead daughter's hand?

FREYDIS: I don't know. I can only think that she would know where to get it.

LAURENCE: And why would she do that?

FREYDIS: You tell me.

PHILIP: She did appear to be upset when she heard that Roger de Blois was married...

LAURENCE: You're improving Philip. Do you think that she meant to do Roger harm?

FREYDIS: I doubt it. She loved him.

LAURENCE: You did nothing to dissuade her from pursuing such a relationship?

FREYDIS: Why should I? She was happy, and so was he. That was all that mattered to me.

PHILIP: Even though you knew that such a union would be frowned on?

FREYDIS: Only by churchmen and snobs.

LAURENCE: And by your own jealous son. He had a problem with the relationship, didn't he?

FREYDIS: He'd never do anything to hurt his sister, and certainly not… that.

LAURENCE: Yes, he was very "protective" of her, shall we say?

FREYDIS: Not protective enough, evidently.

LAURENCE: Did you ever discuss their relationship with Erik?

FREYDIS: No

LAURENCE: And why not?

FREYDIS: You know why.

LAURENCE: Because he wouldn't have got into a furious rage and killed someone?

FREYDIS: No, because he's more patriarchal than the church.

LAURENCE: That must be galling for such a matriarch like you?

FREYDIS: Never mind that. What are you going to do now? Hand them scholars over to the church court?

PHILIP: That will be the proper thing to do. They fall under the church's jurisdiction.

FREYDIS: Where they'll get off with ten Hail Marys and a fine! Christ! The church is full of bloody grace! The town will never stand for it, that's for sure.

LAURENCE: The town will never know.

Laurence lays a purse upon the table.

PHILIP: What's that?

FREYDIS: You telling me to leave town?

LAURENCE: Go and visit your family up North until all this has blown over.

FREYDIS: I haven't got any family up North. What about Erik?

LAURENCE: He will go with you, of course. Make sure you keep him quiet.

FREYDIS: I'm not sure you'll be able to keep Caradoc quiet.

LAURENCE: Caradoc is always full of papal bull, and I'm sure that people will take it as such. What is that infernal din?

Laurence leaps up to look out of the office window. Outside we can hear the sound of people crying, "Hang them! Hang them!" Erik's voice is also audible, crying out "Hang the scholars!"

LAURENCE: How the hell did he get out?

PHILIP: I didn't think he'd killed his own sister, so I let him go.

LAURENCE: You did what? You idiot! Do you want the streets of this town to be streaming with more blood?

PHILIP: Well, it's obvious that the clerks killed the girl, isn't it?

LAURENCE: That is the tale that's being told now, yes, thanks to you!

PHILIP: What are we going to do?

LAURENCE: This is going to require some careful management. I've got to have some time to think. Parade the prisoners on the castle walls on the hour, every hour, and don't open the doors to any priests.

FREYDIS: Am I free to go?

Laurence waves her away.

LAURENCE: Don't leave town. And do whatever you can to cool your son's head.

SCENE 5

Caradoc is leading a crowd of protesters. The crowd repeats each Latin phrase after Caradoc as they walk in circles.

CARADOC: Ab initio, a mensa et thoro, actus reus, ad quod damnum, animus nocendi, casus belli, consensus facit legem, contra bonos mores, de mortuis nil nisi bonum, fiat justitia et pereat mundus, fiat justitia ruat caelum, habeas corpus, hostis humani generis, in articulo mortis, inflagrante delicto, in loco parentis!

One of the protesters stops Caradoc in his tracks.

PROTESTER: Do they actually understand what we're saying? More to the point, can I actually understand what we're saying? Can't we just say: "Down with the Clerks"?

CARADOC: Hmm… It's rather to the point…

The protesters adopt the new chant. Caradoc shrugs and joins in.

PROTESTERS: Down with the clerks! Down with the clerks!

Henry le Coq is being interviewed in Philip's office. Henry is sobbing profusely.

HENRY: I can't believe she's gone. I loved her so much. What happened to her?

LAURENCE: We were rather hoping that you'd be able to tell us.

HENRY: You don't think I had anything to do with it? I -l-loved her.

LAURENCE: How did it happen? You can tell us. You'll have to confess to the church court eventually anyway.

HENRY: I dunno. Maybe Robert hit her when she stole our ale?

LAURENCE: Hit her?

HENRY: Tapped her on the head? It happened so fast. She didn't fall over or anything. And she was still walking and talking.

LAURENCE: Where did this happen?

HENRY: In the High Street. Plenty of people will tell you that Robert hit her and not me.

PHILIP: You do know that we found her in a ditch right outside your lodgings?

HENRY: You did? Maybe she came to see me before she died. I know that she loved me as well. Her eyes told me as much. Oh! If only I had known.

LAURENCE: Let's cut to the case. Which one of you removed her womb?

HENRY: Her w-w-womb? Was she robbed?

LAURENCE: Ever so slightly. You do know what a womb is, don't you?

HENRY: Some kind of purse?

PHILIP: Are you one of de Farnham's clerks?

HENRY: No, we're scholars of the liberal arts.

PHILIP: The liberal arts?

HENRY: Yes, you know, the liberal arts.

LAURENCE: Doesn't sound very practical. Are you practised with the blade?

HENRY: My older brother is more of a s-s-soldier type. Likes to shout somewhat. God knows what he'll make of all this. Oh God, I think I'm going to be sick.

Henry makes retching noises. Once he has finished retching with no result, the questioning resumes.

LAURENCE: What time did you get back to your lodgings last night?

HENRY: I don't know. Maybe one o'clock in the morning.

PHILIP: Is it usual for you to get back so late at night?

HENRY: Well, Robert and I were a bit upset by what happened at the Bear Inn, and so we...

PHILIP: What happened in the Bear?

HENRY: Well, Erika was going to kiss me when that brute of a brother came over and was about to punch me when he starting hitting another scholar instead, and that's when we made our escape. Say, I don't suppose her brother did it, do you suppose? He was always very angry with her.

PHILIP: In what way?

HENRY: Well, he was always shouting at her, grabbing at her. Never leaving her alone. He would scarcely let her breathe. So Erika and I had to grab our moments of intimacy whenever we could, which wasn't often.

LAURENCE: What would happen during these "moments of intimacy"? How would they occur?

HENRY: Well, you know, sometimes she would bend down in front of me to collect the tankards, to reveal some of her womanly flesh. You know to flirt with me. And oftentimes she would smile at me, and look at me in a romantic way. Oh, it's hard to convey how intimate our connection was.

LAURENCE: You don't think that she was just being friendly as she would be to any patron of the inn?

HENRY: Oh no, she would always have a secret smile that was only for me. And she kept a bench warm for us at the very back of the inn. Oh, how I loved her so! And now she's gone.

LAURENCE: What did you do for the rest of the night?

HENRY: Well Robert and I went to various inns on the high street, and I'm afraid that we drank rather too much ale. So much so, that Robert seemed very determined to go to Grope-c-c-c-

PHILIP: I think that we are both aware of that street.

LAURENCE: Speak for yourself, Philip!

PHILIP: So what did you do after that?

HENRY: Well Robert had drunk a bit more than me, and he passed out before we could get to... to... you know, the lane. So, once he roused himself, we made our way back to our lodgings as best we could.

LAURENCE: And you didn't trip up on a corpse along the way?

HENRY: No, thank God. I was practically having to carry him all the way, so bearing his weight took up a great deal of my focus. So I guess Erika must have been left there after we got home.

PHILIP: Did anyone see you on your way back?

HENRY: I don't know, I was too busy trying to hold Robert up.

LAURENCE: What about your fellow lodger, Guy Deschamps? Did you see him before you retired to your bed?

HENRY: No, I didn't. He's a bit of an early bird. Doesn't go out much. Would it be possible for me to see Erika? As a way of saying goodbye to her?

LAURENCE: I'm not sure that's wise. She doesn't exactly smell or look like a bed of roses now. You ever seen a dead body before?

HENRY: N-n-no.

LAURENCE: Do you know Roger de Blois?

HENRY: I don't know him really well. I see him about, but I've never spoken to him. His father is one of my tutors - a very difficult man.

LAURENCE: Would it surprise you to learn that Erika was in a relationship with Roger de Blois?

HENRY: No, that cannot be! She loved me, I tell you! She would never have gone out with that flashy git, she would have seen right through him. No, I think that you're very much mistaken. Besides, his father is very strict and traditional - he would never have a let Roger marry a girl like that!

LAURENCE: A girl like what?

HENRY: Well, you know Erika was very p-p-poor. Roger's father wouldn't have allowed him to marry anyone without wealth.

LAURENCE: But your family would have allowed you to marry her?

HENRY: I don't know about that, but I'm sure I could have come to some arrangement with her. Do you know that several of the masters have courtesans?

LAURENCE: So that's what she would have become? Your whore?

HENRY: Saying it like that makes it sounds seedy. We were in love!

PHILIP: Aren't you training to become a priest?

HENRY: Well yes, but many priests keep… w-w-wives. You know, I've written a treatise against clerical celibacy. Perhaps you would like to read it?

LAURENCE: I'll pass for the moment.

HENRY: I think it's most unhealthy that priests are not allowed to act upon their manly passions…

LAURENCE: Like killing women in the street?

HENRY: Well no. Or perhaps yes. It's perhaps that celibacy allows such impure thoughts to fester in the mind until they explode. Will you let me know if it turns out to be a priest? That could be a most powerful argument in my treatise.

LAURENCE: You'll be amongst the first to know, I assure you.

HENRY: Can I go now?

LAURENCE: We have a few more suspects to question, so we're going to keep you in custody for the moment.

Philip addresses a couple of soldiers.

PHILIP: Take him back to the cells.

The soldiers take Henry away.

PHILIP: Well, what do you think?

LAURENCE: I don't know. The boy seems a little too feeble in both frame and mind to have done it.

PHILIP: Like all of these scholars though, he seems to have the most abject morals.

LAURENCE: As do we all. However, it's hardly in his favour that the body was found directly outside his lodgings.

PHILIP: Do you think that the killer could have placed the body there so as to make Henry look guilty of the crime?

LAURENCE: It's a possibility. Although it's such a public place, I can only think that the girl was killed elsewhere and then dumped there. She was quite a big girl…

PHILIP: So you think it could have been someone with a horse and cart?

LAURENCE: Hmm… Carrying such a corpse would have been difficult for any man otherwise. Then again, while I don't think Henry was capable of killing the girl on her own, he and Robert are more joined at the hip than ever Erik and Erika were. The two of them together, pissed off that Erika had stolen their drink and rejected Henry…

PHILIP: But why dump the body on their own doorstep?

LAURENCE: Too pissed perhaps to make much of an effort to hide the body? Besides, why would they care anyway? They know the church court will merely slap their wrists, seeing as they're training to be clergy.

46

PHILIP: Speaking of which, the church authorities will be knocking on the castle doors very soon.

LAURENCE: Then we'd best placate them by releasing Guy Deschamps. I don't think that he had anything to do with this.

Laurence and Philip lead Guy Deschamps to the castle gates with several soldiers. There is a loud and angry mob outside the gate.

LAURENCE: Are you ready?

GUY: About as ready as I'll ever be.

LAURENCE: Brace yourself. We'll protect you as best we can.

PHILIP: Open the gates!

The soldiers open the gates. Laurence steps forward to address the mob. Erik is amongst them.

LAURENCE: What's the meaning of all this?

ERIK: We demand justice for Erika's murder! What are you going to do about it?

LAURENCE: We are still carrying out our inquiries, which are being hampered by having a mob at the gates. Go back to your homes! There is nothing to see here.

MAN FROM THE CROWD: Isn't that one of the scholars what done this? Let's get him.

The crowd surges towards Guy and the soldiers. Punches are thrown. Philip falls to the ground in his struggle to protect Guy.

ERIK: Leave him alone! He's not one of them.

MAN FROM THE CROWD: He's a scholar alright. Let's hang the bastard!

ERIK: He wasn't one of them, I tell you. It was Henry the Cock and Robert the Cretin who'll hang for this. Let him pass!

The crowd reluctantly stand back and allow Guy, Laurence, Philip and the soldiers to pass. Once they are a safe distance, Erik addresses Caradoc.

ERIK: Do you think they'll let Henry and Robert go too?

CARADOC: No, don't you worry - Philip the Miller will soon bore or grind a confession out of them.

SCENE 8

Philip and Laurence re-enter Philip's office in a flustered state.

PHILIP: That was bloody close! I don't know how we're going to contain them. Unless we send for more men?

LAURENCE: No, I think that would lead to a bloodbath of our fellow townsmen, which would lead to ruin for both of us. No, it's time to take advantage of the King's antagonism to the church.

PHILIP: How do you mean?

LAURENCE: The king's father always railed against the lenity of the church courts. We know for sure that if Henry and Robert go before a church court, then they'll be let off with nothing more than slapped wrists. If such an injustice were to occur, then the townsfolk will rise up against the scholars in vengeance of the bloody murder of one of their own. The King will also see the injustice of such an outcome from the church courts, so I am confident that he will allow us to hang Henry and Robert for murder. If nothing else, this will be a sign that he's serious in his attempts to bring the church to heel.

PHILIP: But we still don't know for sure that they did it.

LAURENCE: Perhaps not. But this town is going to explode if there's not a hanging soon, and many more innocent scholars and townsmen will die.

PHILIP: But if they're innocent... I don't think that would ever rest easy on me.

LAURENCE: I'm not happy with this either. But I just don't see how we're going to get control of this situation otherwise. We have to do this for the greater good. You've seen how angry that crowd is - they're ready to kill. If we do nothing, the bloodbath will also be on our heads. Besides, all of the suspects so far, Henry and Robert are most likely the killers. Justice must be seen to be done.

50

PHILIP: It's with a heavy heart that I agree to this. And, I'm the King's man. If the King commands it, then I will have to obey.

LAURENCE: Very well, it's settled. We'll send a messenger to the King.

SCENE 9

Philip and Laurence enter the Bear Inn, where Erik is clearing tables after a busy night. Caradoc is dozing at a table.

ERIK: If you've come to tell me that you've let them go, there'll be a riot.

Laurence lays a parchment in front of Erik.

ERIK: What's this? A warrant for my arrest?

LAURENCE: No, it's instructions from the King. We are to hang Henry and Robert at dawn.

Erik sits down, surprised.

ERIK: You mean they're not going to the church court?

LAURENCE: The King could not stand for such an injustice, after the bloody murder of such a beloved townswoman.

ERIK: Who's to be the executioner?

LAURENCE: You can be if you like.

ERIK: And I will do it! But I won't be wearing any mask - I want people to see me doing it.

Philip looks uneasy, but Laurence is unperturbed.

LAURENCE: Very well. It would only be fitting that he who was most wronged be the one to carry out the execution. The gallows are being made ready. Come to the castle before first light.

Laurence and Philip exit. Erik rouses Caradoc.

ERIK: You hear that Caradoc? There's going to be a hanging!

SCENE 10

A crowd gathers before the gallows, endlessly crying "Down with clerks! Down with the clerks!" As at the beginning, the gallows are shown as a shadow play. There is a big cheer from the crowd as the silhouettes of Henry and Robert are hung.

ACT 3

SCENE 1

Erik walks in triumph into the Bear Inn. Freydis is busy clearing tables.

ERIK: Well, that was a satisfying morning's work.

FREYDIS: Did you manage to get hold of it?

ERIK: I hid it as you'd told me to.

Caradoc hurries in.

CARADOC: Would you believe it? The rats are leaving the ship! I've never seen so many scholars attempt to mount a horse at the same time. Their technique leaves a lot to be desired. There's so much chaos! They looked like clowns at a fair.

ERIK: Where do you think they're off to?

CARADOC: Some say Paris, others Reading and Cambridge. Although I suspect that those going to Reading are the ones without horses. It'll be amusing to see them walk all that way. Oh, and I've heard that a certain Roger de Blois will be joining his father's cronies in Cambridge.

ERIK: Wow! The town finally free of scholars and clerks!

FREYDIS: We haven't got a moment to lose. Pack your things now!

ERIK: What? Don't you worry, I did what I did on the King's authority. The law's not going to be after me.

FREYDIS: Kings come and kings go. And King John has made more enemies than most. But that's not what I'm concerned about. Now that you've got this hanging out of your system, it's time to chase after the real killer.

ERIK: You don't think Henry and Robert killed her?

FREYDIS: Those dim witted idiots? No, I do not.

ERIK: Then why did you let me hang them?

FREYDIS: Because the town would have exploded with rage if you had not. And now the killer will think that they've gotten away with it, so they won't be expecting us to chase after them.

CARADOC: So who do you think it was?

FREYDIS: One of them scholars. It was obviously the work of a learned man.

ERIK: So how do we track them down now that they've gone to the four corners of the Earth?

CARADOC: Maybe you could do what they did in the Bible?

ERIK: Turn the other cheek? No way!

CARADOC: No, I was thinking about the Battle of Gibeah in the Book of Judges. One day, a Levite was travelling in the country of the tribe of Benjamin, Gibeah, with his concubine. Night was falling, so he decided to stay the night instead of travelling onto Jerusalem. Now the people of Gibeah were decidedly unfriendly, apart from one hospitable old man, who invited them to stay. It wasn't long after nightfall that the ruffians of the town began to knock on the door of their lodgings, demanding that they be allowed to rape the Levite.

ERIK: They wanted to rape a man?

CARADOC: I know it sounds bizarre, but there are similar tales in the Bible. Like in Sodom and Gomorrah, where the mob wanted to rape the angels that were staying with Lot. Hospitality was very important in the Holy Land, so raping a male guest would be about the worst thing that any disreputable mob could do. The Gibeah mob probably just wanted to rob the Levite. Anyway, the Levite got so fed up with mob banging on the door, that he took his concubine and threw her out to them. When morning came, the mob dispersed, and the Levite went to fetch his concubine. She didn't move when he called her name, so he gave her a little kick, and was most dismayed to discover that the mob had ravished her so much that she had died.

FREYDIS: You left out the beginning of the story, where the concubine ran away from him, and so the Levite went to her father's house and basically bribed the father into letting him take back as his concubine. Which makes me think that this is a true story, as the concubine knew that the Levite was a bad one from the start.

ERIK: What's this got to do with our situation?

CARADOC: Well, the Levite was so miffed at this outrageous hospitality that he cut up the concubine's body, and sent the pieces to the other Jewish tribes as evidence so that they would rise up against the tribe of Benjamin. And this is what they did, for the tribe of Benjamin was wiped off the face of the Earth in the resulting battle of Gibeah.

ERIK: You want me to cut up Erika's body?

CARADOC: If you want to wipe the scholars off the face of the Earth… Look, all I'm saying is that this is what they did in the Good Book.

ERIK: Damn what they did in the Bible! I'm not going to cut Erika up! Get the hell out of here!

Erik chases Caradoc out of the inn, and returns a few moments later, panting from the exertion.

FREYDIS: Never mind Caradoc's whimsies, there are more subtle ways to achieve our aims.

ERIK: Such as?

56

FREYDIS: The man that killed Erika fears the other. You must go to the other place, and become what this man fears.

ERIK: Other place? What other place? Do you mean Cambridge or Paris? It's bad enough crossing the road in this wintry weather, let alone the sea.

Laurence enters.

FREYDIS: Do you have the money?

LAURENCE: Aye, but are you really sure you want to sell up?

FREYDIS: We're not coming back.

ERIK: Speak for yourself. What about Mathilda and the child?

FREYDIS: The love of your life is coming with us.

ERIK: I'm not sure she'll like that.

FREYDIS: She wants me to deliver the child and no one else, so that's her choice.

LAURENCE: You sure you want to give this place up? There's a lot of history in here.

FREYDIS: And there'll be many more years of history.

LAURENCE: Very well.

Laurence hands Freydis a contract, who quickly reads through it.

FREYDIS: I see that I'm selling to your wife. Very wise.

LAURENCE: She's always had her eye on this land as you know. Although I'm afraid that she wants to tear down the current building, and create something more permanent. You don't mind do you?

FREYDIS: I'm not one for standing in the way of progress.

Freydis is about to sign, but Erik takes the contract off her. However, it's evident that he cannot read its contents, so he hands it back to his mother.

FREYDIS: You could do with some scholarly learning Erik.

ERIK: Learning hasn't done this town's scholars any good. How much are you going to give us for this?

FREYDIS: Enough to get us a donkey to transport Mathilda.

ERIK: What? That's robbery!

Erik looks threateningly at Laurence.

FREYDIS: Calm down, Erik! Besides, it's all thanks to you two that the price of transport has suddenly gone up in this town.

ERIK: You mean that you and I are going to have to walk all that way in this weather?

FREYDIS: Plenty of scholars will be without horses too. What's good enough for them pansies will be good enough for us too. Remember that you're of Danish blood, Erik.

ERIK: As if I could ever forget.

LAURENCE: Are you sure you'll be alright on the road?

FREYDIS: I've got Erik to look after me.

ERIK: Not that I did that so well for Erika.

FREYDIS: You're not done in that task yet. We'll do right by Erika, don't you worry.

LAURENCE: Let me know if I can be of any assistance.

FREYDIS: We'll be fine. But you'd better watch your back, Laurence. There are still scholars in this town, no matter what the King says, and they won't forget what happened in a hurry.

LAURENCE: Pity you won't get to see the town free of scholars.

FREYDIS: Mark my words, they'll be back in a few years' time, and merchants like you will welcome them with open arms.

LAURENCE: I'll be damned if we get those bloody foreigners back!

FREYDIS: No, you merchants will soon miss the scholars' silver, and the mighty prices you charge them, which will cause a riot in a hundred years and more, when the scholars get fed up with being ripped off. But that's another story. Come on now Erik, let's be packing! We haven't a moment to lose.

Laurence walks into Philip's office. Philip gets up and pours some wine into a tankard.

LAURENCE: What's this? Celebrating the clerks' departure already?

PHILIP: For relief, if nothing else. It's been a long day. Do you want some?

LAURENCE: Don't mind if I do.

Philip pours some wine into another tankard for Laurence.

LAURENCE: Where's the blade gone?

PHILIP: Hmm?

LAURENCE: The blade that killed the girl - it's gone!

Both of them look for it in the desk drawers. After a thorough search, Philip gives up.

PHILIP: Does it matter?

LAURENCE: I guess not. There's nothing we can really do with it, now that it's done its bloody work.

There is a knock on the door and a guard enters.

GUARD: Sorry Sir, but he insisted…

PHILIP: What?

William de Blois strides imperiously into the office.

WILLIAM: Well Gentlemen, I hope you satisfied with the nasty business that you have conducted.

LAURENCE: You do know that the King has ordered the scholars to leave town?

WILLIAM: Oh, woe betide me if I should disobey orders from a King! Don't worry, I shall be leaving town soon, and I will kick the town's dust from off my feet as I leave.

LAURENCE: Good to hear that we won't be blessed by your ugly mug for much longer.

WILLIAM: Oh, how the King's backing makes you bold! You won't be smirking when you are judged. And you will be judged sooner than you think!

LAURENCE: We won't be judged by the likes of you no more.

WILLIAM: Everyone complains about how soft the church courts are! But you will wish that you were judged by the church when you face justice. No, you will face judgement from a higher power. Besides, who were you to judge those boys? You knew that they were innocent.

LAURENCE: We did what we had to do to prevent more bloodshed. You know how ugly the mood in this town is. You should be thanking us for averting that.

WILLIAM: Yes, but I'm sure that someone with more endeavour than you two would have got to the truth and found the real murderer.

LAURENCE: Do you have any information that could lead us to such a suspect?

There is a sudden cacophony outside the office, with repeated shouts of "Justice for Robert and Henry! Justice for Robert and Henry!" Guy de Champs and some other scholars try to burst their way into to the office, but are held back by guards.

LAURENCE: What is it with the guards today? Are they intent on letting everyone in?

Philip and Laurence depart the office to deal with the disturbance. While they are absent, William pours a black liquid into Laurence's tankard, and gives it a twirl so that the contents will mix. After a few moments, Laurence re-enters.

LAURENCE: We've had to give some shoe leather to some more of your clerks.

Laurence takes a long swig from his tankard.

WILLIAM: You'll be relieved to hear that from today, you'll never see the likes of us scholars again.

LAURENCE: That is indeed good to hear.

WILLIAM: No, you'll never see your superiors again where you're going. But we'll be looking down, laughing at you from our heavenly pastures. Farewell Laurence Kepeharm, shame that you couldn't keep yourself or those scholars from harm.

William leaves. Laurence shrugs.

LAURENCE: Whatever.

Laurence then begins to feel uneasy, and loosens his collar. He stands up and walks to the door, beginning to choke.

LAURENCE: Whatever… Whatever have you done to me? Call the Gar!

Laurence collapses.

Erik, Freydis and Mathilda are gathered around a campfire.

ERIK: One day in, and already I'm bloody freezing.

MATHILDA: And there was me thinking that you were a Dane.

ERIK: What is this other place you're talking about mother? Walking all the way to Cambridge is bad enough. Is it related to one of your prophecies? I don't know what the use of prophecy is if you can see hundreds of years into the future, but can't see what's happening next Thursday. Your prophecies didn't stop Erika being killed.

FREYDIS: But they may lead us to her killer.

ERIK: So what is this other place, if not Cambridge?

MATHILDA: When she talks of another place, she's not talking of an actual place, dopey!

ERIK: So what does she mean? Why can't you spit it out, mother?

MATHILDA: She means that you must shave off your beard, and become a lady like me.

ERIK: Huh? That's the daftest thing I've heard all day.

MATHILDA: With your long blonde locks, you could very well be a lady.

ERIK: Get off!

MATHILDA: Indeed, I oftentimes thought that Erika was you, and you was Erika from behind.

ERIK: Well, we were twins.

MATHILDA: One day, I even squeezed Erika's buttock because I thought she was you. She nearly punched me!

ERIK: Yeah well, I seem to see her everywhere myself nowadays. Every woman with blonde hair becomes her for an instant.

FREYDIS: Me too son. I know you loved your sister, too much really, but you didn't really understand her. That's what I'm getting at. To find Erika's killer, you must feel like her.

ERIK: I do feel for her, ma! This is really tearing me apart!

FREYDIS: I know. But you need to know how she felt.

ERIK: Wouldn't it be better just to keep to tracing the killer's steps? It's he we need to understand and discover, not her.

FREYDIS: But to do that, we need to understand what he fears. And he fears women.

ERIK: Erika would be enough to scare any man, I grant you that.

FREYDIS: Yes, many a man fears a powerful woman in a patriarchy, where men think they rule. Such men feel that they need to put powerful women in their place, to force them into being nothing but objects of desire and pleasure.

ERIK: I don't know what you mean mother, I really don't.

MATHILDA: She means that you must become an object of desire and pleasure too, Erik. You have an almost feminine beauty…

ERIK: That's enough of that!

MATHILDA: All right, let's put it into manly terms that you may understand. Your mother needs bait to reel the killer in, and you're the spitting image of your sister. If the killer sees you all dolled up, it should be enough to take his breath away… For here, living and breathing is a woman he's already killed! And most men have a type of woman they fancy. I bet a killer like that would be most specific in his tastes.

ERIK: And when he tries to do his bit?

MATHILDA: He'll be most surprised to find a real man who'll cut off his dick!

FREYDIS: The killer will indeed find you to be a most uncanny surprise!

ERIK: Well, if you put it that way…

FREYDIS: But to be really convincing, you'll have to walk and talk like a woman, and experience womanly things.

MATHILDA: In other words, you'll have to earn your keep by helping us with the midwifery.

ERIK: Well, if it helps capture Erika's killer… I guess I'll have to stomach it.

MATHILDA: And it will help you prepare for your own upcoming fatherhood.

ERIK: As if I could forget!

SCENE 4

Mathilda, Freydis and Erik are attending on a woman (Rosie) who is giving birth and screaming in agony. Erik is wearing women's clothing.

ERIK: Shall I fetch the Crane's foot now?

ROSIE: We've already done that bit, you silly wench!

ERIK: Shall I open the windows and drawers?

ROSIE: The windows are always open, and I don't have any drawers except those that you've taken off already. What do think this place is? The palace of Westminster? Where'd you get this silly moo?

MATHILDA: Apologies ma'am, this is Erika's first day of training.

ROSIE: Is she going to be sick? God, I hope she's not going to be sick. I don't want any but my bodily mess on this here pristine bed sheets.

FREYDIS: She's not going to be sick. She's stronger than she looks.

MATHILDA: Would she believe she's of Danish stock?

ROSIE: That I would not, although her face is as streaky as a rash of bacon. She's not going to faint on me now, is she?

FREYDIS: She'll be fine.

ROSIE: Only I wouldn't want to put her off for life, if this be her chosen profession. So, this is your first baby love?

ERIK: Yes.

ROSIE: Well, I hope it's not your last. There's plenty more where that came from.

Erik waves the crane foot.

66

ERIK: Is this thing working? You sure you don't want me to get another one?

ROSIE: Right you are, there's another crane on the roof, come to deliver my baby in a fine linen cloth. Be sure to bring that babe with you while you rip that bloody foot from the crane.

MATHILDA: No need to be sarky Rosie.

ROSIE: Well this Erika don't seem to have seen lady's bits before, despite her being a lady. I hope the plan was for a long apprenticeship. God!

ERIK: Just keep breathing.

ROSIE: What do think I'm doing, you ninny! Ah! Don't you know any spells girl?

ERIK: Ave Maria…

ROSIE: I asked for a spell, not a bloody prayer! It looks like you haven't got a bloody prayer of becoming a midwife! Besides, I don't think calling on the holy virgin will help, 'cos I ain't much like her. Never learn my bloody lesson, do I? This will be the fifth one. Never mind "Hail Mary": I bet she was full of grace when Jesus skipped into the manger! You're looking a bit peaky again - you're sure you're not in pain? Can I get you some water from the well?

ERIK: I'll be fine.... Oh.

Erik faints.

ROSIE: I don't think she's quite cut for the family business. Let's hope that she never gets in the family's way! What is it?

FREYDIS: You have a beautiful baby girl.

ROSIE: Ah… She's a strong one! What mighty lungs eh? Don't think

67

I'll be calling her Erika!

SCENE 5

Erik strolls onto the stage in a drunken state. He is wearing men's clothing again. Freydis and Mathilda come in from the opposite direction.

FREYDIS: There you are! I was worried frantic.

ERIK: No need to bother, mother, as you can see, I am fine.

MATHILDA: Not a little worse for wear though.

ERIK: I've had a merry few, I'll admit that.

FREYDIS: Now I see why you wanted to divert to the Icknield Way. You know Royston's not far from Cambridge.

MATHILDA: So why aren't you wearing your womanly dress no more? You'll give the game away.

ERIK: I don't care anymore. I've stopped doing that... that...

MATHILDA: But you know that wearing women's clothing, and acting like a woman is integral to the plan!

ERIK: I don't care. I'm not wearing a dress no more. I'll find the killer my own way.

FREYDIS: And what way is that?

ERIK: Never you mind, mother.

MATHILDA: Aw! Is our big strong Dane ashamed that he fainted?

ERIK: I did not faint! I just fell over, that's all.

FREYDIS: Don't worry. It's natural to feel a little sick the first time that you see nature in action. But you'll soon get used to it.

ERIK: I don't want to get used to it. It's not natural for a man to be there at the birth… unless they be a…

FREYDIS: Surgeon. Yes, well thank God I've never had the need to call on one of them butchers.

Erik has managed to doze off while sitting in the middle of the street.

FREYDIS: You've dozed in a most propitious place, I'll give you that. Mathilda, go fetch me a rope from the donkey.

Mathilda goes off to get the rope, while Freydis opens a hatch. She peers into it with a lantern.

FREYDIS: So the stories were true! I bow down to you, most august Augustinians!

Mathilda comes back with the rope.

MATHILDA: What's that you found, mother?

Freydis glares at her.

MATHILDA: -in-law

Freydis keeps glaring at her.

MATHILDA: -to-be.

FREYDIS: It's a cave with the most mystical of paintings. Help me lower him into it.

MATHILDA: Huh? I don't think Erik's really into artwork.

FREYDIS: You want to sober him up, don't you? Well, this should scare the wits out of him.

Mathilda ties the rope around Erik's waist and pulls him to his feet. Erik is still dozing.

MATHILDA: You sure I ought to be doing this in my condition?

FREYDIS: You'll be fine. Now help me lower him down.

Freydis and Mathilda lower Erik down through the hatch.

Erik is lying on the floor, asleep. He gradually begins to stir.

ERIK: God! This has got to be the worst lodgings so far! Did you manage to find the only inn with no fire, mother! I expect even the manger was more comfortable than this. Did you also manage to find the only inn with no candles, mother?

Mathilda and Freydis are offstage.

FREYDIS: You want a light boy? Here you go!

A lantern lands on the floor next to Erik. Erik grabs it, but then is startled to see a kaleidoscope of images from the Royston cave projected onto the theatre screen. Erik is frightened by the monstrous images as he swirls around, desperately seeking the exit.

ERIK: Aargh! I can't find my way out - get me out of here.

Freydis and Mathilda come onto the stage and "pull" Erik from the cave.

FREYDIS: How does it feel to be born again?

ERIK: Never do that to me again, you crazy old hag!

MATHILDA: What on Earth did you see down there?

ERIK: All kinds of crazy images - mostly saints and soldiers. There was one picture of a woman with the biggest pussy you'll ever see! Truly sickening it was.

FREYDIS: You can see images like that on any church. We'll give you some womb envy yet.

ERIK: I'm not putting on another dress, no matter what you say mother.

FREYDIS: You want to go back down the hole?

ERIK: No, I'm never going back there again.

MATHILDA: Well then, you're going to have to wear the bloody dress.

FREYDIS: Don't worry son, you'll have plenty of time to grow into it, as I suspect we won't find the killer that soon. And you'll have expert teachers in Mathilda and me.

ERIK: I guess.

FREYDIS: We'll be a bit more gentle this time. I wasn't expecting any midwifery work on the road.

ERIK: Just as long as we don't bump into anyone I know.

Erik relents with a sigh, and gets into the dress. He and Mathilda leave the stage.

FREYDIS: Don't you worry. We won't see anyone we know… Except the killer perhaps.

SCENE 7

Erik, Freydis and Mathilda in their simple Cambridge home. Mathilda is evidently pregnant now with a baby bump.

ERIK: Ah God, morning already? I didn't sleep a wink last night. My back is killing me.

MATHILDA: Well, as long as it's not as bad as Mr Killingback's, you'll be fine.

FREYDIS: Don't forget to put on your womanly voice for when the punters arrive.

ERIK: Don't worry ma, most folks reckon I just have a deep voice.

MATHILDA: Which all of the lads find very sexy!

ERIK: They do not! Don't talk rot!

MATHILDA: How are your piles this morning, dear?

ERIK: For the last time, I do not have womb envy!

FREYDIS: The French will call it couvade: sympathetic pregnancy.

MATHILDA: So that's why he was vomiting so much during the early days of my pregnancy!

ERIK: Bad ale, that's all that was.

MATHILDA: It looks like you've sunk a few ales, judging from that belly!

FREYDIS: Yes, you really ought to keep in shape. Some of the lads won't find you so alluring if they think that you're pregnant. You've got to look your best today. It's the start of the Midsummer Fair.

ERIK: So, we've been here six months already, and we're still no closer to finding Erika's killer.

MATHILDA: All sorts come to the fair, from far and wide. It may well attract the killer.

ERIK: It'll probably be some kind of killer clown or lute player, knowing my luck.

MATHILDA: No doubt. Right, I'm off. Mrs Doggett looks like she's about to pop. And speaking of killing backs, here's your first customer of the day.

Mathilda exits, and Richard Woodnutt comes in.

ERIK: How's the head today, Woodnutt? Is it feeling particularly wooden?

RICHARD: What? I've not been drinking, if that's what you mean, nor am I'm likely to.

FREYDIS: Your diagnosis won't work on him, as he's not from round here. I believe the Woodnutts are originally from Cheshire?

RICHARD: That's right.

FREYDIS: And your family now owns a mill in Trumpington?

RICHARD: Again right. Where is this leading?

FREYDIS: Don't ever let any of your brood marry a clergyman's daughter.

RICHARD: Huh?

ERIK: Don't ever have anything to do with the clergy, or any of the damn scholars in this town.

FREYDIS: And don't ever rip off any of these new colleges, as that will lead to the most sordid tale that will live on through the

75

generations.

RICHARD: What are you the hell are you suggesting? I'm an honest man. Look, the reason why I came here is to warn you that I don't want any trouble at the fair tonight.

ERIK: What kind of trouble?

RICHARD: Any kind of trouble. We traders fear that if there's any whiff of scandal, then Barnwell Priory will finally succeed in getting the fair's charter from King John.

ERIK: That would put a bummer on things.

RICHARD: Indeed. I swear that that snooty Barnwell Chronicler is already sniffing about. Hopefully he'll sniff too close to that bloody leper chapel. Just look at what's happening with the fair that they put on!

FREYDIS: You've no need to worry about us. We're squeaky clean here.

ERIK: Except when we're covered in afterbirth.

RICHARD: Yes, well I'll leave you to your business. Good day to you.

Richard exits, and Mr Killingback comes in.

ERIK: How are you Killingback?

KILLINGBACK: I'm in agony! I can hardly move, thanks to this bloody back! Oh, why was I cursed to be born into the family of Killingback?

ERIK: You can't help your family inheritance and the tall lanky build you got from them, but maybe there are other things that you can do to help your back problem.

KILLINGBACK: Such as?

ERIK: Well, you could change your profession. Being an agricultural labourer doesn't help your back at all.

KILLINGBACK: Farm work is all I know how to do. I'd love to be a blacksmith, but banging all that heavy metal won't do my back or my hearing any good.

ERIK: You could become a scholar. I hear it's all the rage nowadays.

KILLINGBACK: I know nothing of letters. Besides, I don't have enough money to sit on my arse doing nothing all day.

ERIK: Let me have a look at your back.

Killingback rolls up his shirt.

ERIK: I see the problem. Your spine is quite knotted from your bad posture.

KILLINGBACK: Is there any cure for it?

Erik hands him a small jar.

ERIK: Ask your wife to rub this ointment on your back daily. This should get rid of the pain after a while.

KILLINGBACK: Many thanks, Ma'am. Have this loaf of bread for your troubles.

ERIK: Who's next? Aw, Mrs Casburn I see. What's wrong this time?

Killingback exits, and Mrs Casburn comes in.

CASBURN: I burnt my hand cooking dinner last night. Look, see how it smarts so.

ERIK: Mmm, that does look bad.

FREYDIS: Don't you or your family ever go to Burwell.

CASBURN: What?

FREYDIS: They burn well at Burwell.

CASBURN: Oh well, thanks for that Freydis. I'll look out for that sort of… thing.

ERIK: Don't mind mother - she's going to be reading palms at the fair tonight.

CASBURN: I'd go myself, 'cept I'm scared at all that fire eating. Well, what's to be done for it?

Erik hands her a small jar.

ERIK: Rub this ointment on the wound twice daily, and it'll get better in no time.

CASBURN: Many thanks Erika. Perhaps you'd like this jar of Casburn Burner ale? I brewed it specially for the fair.

Erik opens the jar and gives a sniff.

ERIK: Very fruity, I'm sure all the family will enjoy that. See you at the fair.

Casburn exits, and Mr Badcock enters.

BADCOCK: I'm the last of this morning's queue.

ERIK: Dare I ask what troubles you, Badcock?

Badcock reaches into his trousers.

BADCOCK: Well I….

ERIK: I don't need to see it! Just describe what the problem is.

Badcock gets a cucumber and puts it on the table.

BADCOCK: No need to look alarmed ma'am, I was just going to give you that.

ERIK: Well?

BADCOCK: It's just that the fella downstairs... He keeps bleeding when I wee, and I want to wee all the time. I ain't been sleeping around.

ERIK: With your looks and your reputation, I can well believe that. Now, Badcock, do you recall what I told you last time?

BADCOCK: About the best way of wiping my arse?

ERIK: Yes.

BADCOCK: About wiping the shit away from my fella downstairs and not towards him?

ERIK: Yes?

BADCOCK: But it's so hard when you've been doing it the other way all your life!

ERIK: Well, just use the pain that you're currently in as a reminder. And don't forget - you shouldn't use the same thing you used to wipe your shit to dry... the fella downstairs.

BADCOCK: Don't use the same thing to wipe my shit to dry the fella downstairs... I think I've got it.

ERIK: In fact, it's best not to dry... the fella downstairs at all. Just shake it about to get the drips off.

BADCOCK: Right you are. Do you have anything to reduce the pain?

Erik hands Badcock a small jar.

ERIK: Mix a pinch of this powder with your ale four times a day, and you'll feel better in no time.

BADCOCK: Thanks Erika. Please take that vegetable in payment. I was going to enter it into competition at the fair, as it's my prize one.

ERIK: Many thanks.

BADCOCK: And I'll tell you this for nought. Do you know the easy way to grow vegetables that large?

ERIK: No, please tell me.

BADCOCK: You pee on them!

ERIK: Great. I'll bear that in mind next time I want to grow a prize winning vegetable. How's Mrs. Badcock?

BADCOCK: Ah, your ma will tell you she's doing fine.

ERIK: Have you decided on what you'll call your new arrival?

BADCOCK: Don't tell the missus, but I was thinking of calling it Ivor. Get it?

ERIK: Ivor Badcock. Mmm. Well, it may be true, but is that the kind of name that you ought to afflict your child with?

BADCOCK: It never did me any harm! You going to the fair Erika?

ERIK: Yeah. Would you mind if I entered your vegetable into competition?

BADCOCK: That would do me proud! See you later.

Badcock exits.

FREYDIS: What? Don't you want to eat Badcock's cucumber?

ERIK: I think it might spoil my appetite... completely.

FREYDIS: You're doing well with your patients.

ERIK: You think?

FREYDIS: Well, they wouldn't come keep coming back if they were not satisfied.

ERIK: Still, this must be the easiest town in the world to be a physician. I know what everyone's ailments are just from their names!

Erik and Freydis are wandering around Midsummer Fair. There are jugglers, musicians, clowns, acrobats, and merchants selling goods. Eventually, the stage gets darker and quieter as night falls.

ERIK: Well, I don't know what you were expecting. The killer's obviously a no-show.

FREYDIS: Don't give up hope just yet. Look, here's Doggett.

Mr. Doggett runs up to them.

ERIK: What are you doing here at the fair Mr Doggett? Keeping out of your wife's way while she delivers?

DOGGETT: It's not that. It's your sister!

ERIK: Mathilda? What's wrong?

DOGGETT: I've been told that it's her waters that have broken, not my wife's.

ERIK: Shit! I'll be right there.

FREYDIS: No, you wait here Erika. I'll handle this. You don't want to be missing the fair.

ERIK: Sod the fair! This is my chi… sister we're talking about.

FREYDIS: Don't you worry Erika! I've handled many a double child bearing in my time. And Mathilda knows what to do. No, you stay at the fair, or you'll not hear the end of it. You go on ahead Doggett.

Doggett exits.

ERIKA: Ma! You know the one advantage of this dress thing is that it meant that I could attend…

FREYDIS: I wouldn't have come up with the idea if I'd known that it would make you so soppy! You know men aren't allowed. Hsst! We're very close now, I feel it, so don't muck this up. Besides, you know that I can keep things going until you're back. This may be our only chance - we must take it!

ERIK: Alright, just as long as you keep your end of the bargain - I want to be there when the babe arrives.

FREYDIS: Keep that cloak around you - the night's getting cold. And we'll unfurl some more of your golden locks.

ERIK: Hope I don't just attract perverts like last time.

FREYDIS: Just the right pervert, we hope! Have you got the chain on securely?

ERIK: Aye. You never did tell me where you got it from?

FREYDIS: Never mind that, there's work to be done. I'll give your love to Mathilda, shall I?

ERIK: If you think that it will help, then sure.

FREYDIS: Right, well, be on your guard. Remember that you're a Dane!

ERIK: As if I could ever forget! Be gone with you, and leave me with the dregs of the fair.

Freydis hurriedly departs.

Erik wanders forlornly through the fair. There's very little entertainment left, except for staggering drunks. Roger de Blois calls out off stage.

ROGER: Erika! Erika! Is that you?

Roger arrives on stage, staggering slightly, as he's obviously drunk a little too much. He looks quite bedraggled, and now sports a rough beard.

ROGER: It is you! I knew the old bastard was lying when he said you'd been killed. Thank God! You don't know what torments I've been through. Why didn't you come sooner?

ERIK: And what old bastard would that be?

ROGER: Erika? Erik?

Erik gathers Roger into a neck hold.

ERIK: Yes, it's me. I ought to kill you right now! I know it was you who murdered her!

ROGER: You mean she is dead? God! When I saw you just now, I thought that you were her. Oh God! I had hoped and dreamed that she was still alive…

ERIK: Well, she's not! You made bloody sure of that all right.

Roger suddenly slumps. Erik startled, releases his hold.

ROGER: What are you waiting for? Kill me now. You know you've always wanted to.

Erik freezes.

ROGER: Kill me, damn you! Life's not worth living, now I know for sure Erika's dead.

ERIK: I'll take you to the sheriff.

ROGER: What for? My father says you hung two men of Oxford. Just kill me now. I don't want to live any more.

ERIK: You must face justice!

ROGER: I don't care for any of that. All I know is that Erika's dead. I bet the old bastard did it himself. So just kill me in his place.

ERIK: Why did you always hate me?

ROGER: This again? For God's sake, I was just mucking about when we were kids. The old bastard told me that you were a dog that could be kicked, so I kicked you. It was just play fighting. You never did have a sense of humour.

ERIK: But why did Erika egg you on and take your side?

ROGER: She was always a bit older than you, although you're the same age. She just wanted to be her own person, but you were so bloody possessive and jealous! You could never let her go.

ERIK: And I was right! Look what happened to her!

ROGER: You may have been right, this one case in a hundred thousand. But that doesn't mean that you were right you treat her like you did, just because of one freak accident.

ERIK: There was no accident! You ripped open her womb to kill her baby!

ROGER: She was with child? God!

ERIK: Well no, but you weren't to know that.

ROGER: The bastard cut open her womb?

ERIK: Yes!

ROGER: You think that I could ever do that to Erika? I loved her! No, this is the work of some monster, some monster that hates women. Aargh!

Roger cries out as he is stabbed to death by a hooded assailant. In the struggle, the killer's hood falls away to reveal Caradoc.

ERIK: What the hell did you do that for?

CARADOC: Well, I dunno about you, but I find that a little bit of Midsummer murder helps pass the time. Well, aren't you going to say how-do as you walk through the fair?

ERIK: What?

CARADOC: Never mind. It's not just your mother that's prescient.

ERIK: What the hell are you doing here?

CARADOC: Is this the way to greet one of your old muckers?

ERIK: Why did you kill him? I thought we were getting somewhere.

CARADOC: Keep your voice down! You looked like you were going to kill him, so I saved you the bother, that's all. And after what he did to poor Erika, it's all he deserved.

ERIK: But I don't think he did it. What on earth are you doing here? Are you ever at that friary of yours'?

CARADOC: This is one of the biggest fairs in the kingdom. The friar sent me to see if I could do a little business. Well, at least I persuaded that would be a good idea. He likes any excuse to send me out and about. Reckons I would send all the other monks mad otherwise. And you really don't want that many mad monks around.

ERIK: But why did you have to kill him? That's hardly the action of a man of god.

CARADOC: This? Don't worry about this. A hundred Hail Marys will fix this, a thousand at most. The church courts are, by their nature, very forgiving.

ERIK: But how did you know how to thrust your blade like that?

CARADOC: You know nothing of me before I became a friar. All people see nowadays is the monkly habit. They know nothing of the raging passions within.

ERIK: What raging passions?

CARADOC: Before I was a friar, I was a killer of men.

ERIK: What?

CARADOC: Like a certain other Welsh monk that I could mention, I was a soldier before I was a friar.

ERIK: So you became a monk because you couldn't handle all the killing?

CARADOC: No, I could handle the killing fine. Never bothered me. It's just that when you're a soldier, people expect you to kill, and well, they never really knew the real me. But now I'm a monk, people notice a bit more when I slaughter them. "But you're a man of God!" they cry with that delicious look of horror on their face.

ERIK: Ha ha ha! Very funny Caradoc. You almost had me going. Now help me move the body before we're discovered.

CARADOC: And do what with it?

ERIK: Throw it into the river.

CARADOC: Into the mighty fast flowing waters of the Cam? Why not give the august Augustinians a surprise by leaving him in their cellar? That's not too far away.

ERIK: Yeah right. Look, you might face a church court, but William De Blois will have me hang.

CARADOC: Hanging an innocent man? I'm sure that would never happen in this day and age!

ERIK: Don't remind me. Well, are you going to help or what?

CARADOC: Why not? It'll help pass the time.

Erik is bent over the body. Caradoc moves forward as if to help, but then rushes forward and stabs Erik in the side. In the struggle, they both fall over Roger's body. Erik manages to prevent Caradoc from stabbing him again. Caradoc lies over Erik, trying to stab him again, but Erik has a firm grip on his arms.

ERIK: What the hell are you doing?

CARADOC: Sorry, it's nothing personal, but killing Roger has rather fired up the demon inside. Besides, I'm curious to see if you'll bleed like Erika.

ERIK: You... You killed Erika? Why?

CARADOC: Don't you know? Wretches like you are mostly murdered by people they know. I blame you personally. You've got victim stamped all over you.

ERIK: I am a Dane!

CARADOC: Really? You look more like a dame to me. My mistake. Let me cut you up and see if there really is a prick in there.

Suddenly another figure rushes out of the darkness and skewers Caradoc with a blade. When satisfied with her work, Freydis pulls down her hood.

FREYDIS: What about that little prick? You made a mistake alright! To think that you could fool a dame and a Dane like me.

CARADOC: Ah, I see my little ruse didn't work?

FREYDIS: Mathilda was never going to bear child early, and Mrs Doggett's still a good few days off.

CARADOC: You're a callous one. Putting your only surviving child out for bait to the angel of death.

FREYDIS: I've born hundreds of babes, not just this one. Besides, did you not hear a chink as you stabbed him?

CARADOC: I rather presumed I hit her purse.

FREYDIS: He's wearing chainmail. I would have thought that an old soldier like you would recognise that.

CARADOC: How did you ever afford that? On your back, I presume?

Erik viciously kicks Caradoc.

CARADOC: Wow! Steady on boygirl! You nearly killed me!

ERIK: That was the point. Why did you kill Erika, you bastard? She saw you as the father she never had.

CARADOC: She did? Well, I wish I'd known. It would have made killing her all the more delightful.

Erik kicks Caradoc again.

CARADOC: Steady on! I think your mother's done most of the hard work, as per usual.

ERIK: Why'd you do it?

CARADOC: Don't you recall all those lurid tales I told about women from the Bible? The really juicy bits from the Good Book? Well, they really gripped my interest from a young age, opened my horizons, and increased my appetite so that it encompassed all sorts of unholy goods.

ERIK: Why-did-you-do-it?

CARADOC: I did it because I enjoyed it.

ERIK: What?

CARADOC: No other reason than that. I did it because it was fun.

Erik kicks Caradoc again.

CARADOC: You kick away. I feel nothing.

FREYDIS: You've never felt anything at all, have you, you wretch?

CARADOC: Your mother understands. I knew she would.

ERIK: Well, I don't understand, and I'll never understand how you could kill one of your own.

CARADOC: But that's it, you see. I know you - I've known you your whole life, and yet I feel absolutely nothing at all for you. I see someone fall down in the street, and I don't care. Some people laugh at that, and others cry, but me - nothing.

FREYDIS: There's nothing but an aching void inside of you.

CARADOC: Whereas you Erik are too full of useless passion that does no good for anyone. But I'm not quite an empty vessel when it comes to passion, for I have an appetite for ripping flesh.

ERIK: But why? Where does it come from?

CARADOC: You could call it the voice of God that impels me to punish the wicked and the sinful.

FREYDIS: You'd do good to rip out your own flesh, for there's none so sinful as you!

CARADOC: Yes, it was the voice of God, impelling me to remove whores from the streets.

Freydis pushes Erik out of the way and kicks Caradoc herself.

FREYDIS: That's the lie you monsters will always make.

CARADOC: What can I say? People feel better if they think that there was a moral imperative behind such random slaughter. They don't understand that the kill is the thrill.

ERIK: There's nothing moral about what you did!

CARADOC: Keep up, you Dame Dane, I already surpassed that. Well, at least the likes of William de Blois will now admire me for doing what they dared not to.

ERIK: Even after you killed his son?

CARADOC: I'm sure he'll forgive me in time. He's also a man with a dark heart, like me.

FREYDIS: You always despised the scholars, didn't you? That's why you left Erika outside their lodgings.

CARADOC: Bastards always looked down on me. But I know more about the dank, dark recesses of the Bible than they'll ever know. Perhaps I still have time to expel them from this town also. Let me know if a mangy Doggett barks by, won't you?

ERIK: We'll do no such thing!

CARADOC: Ach! I don't have much time left, thanks to you, Mother Freydis. But at least I'll go down in history as Caradoc the Killer! You will write to Philip the Miller, won't you, and let him know that it was me that dunnit, won't you? I know that you have some learning.

FREYDIS: We'll do no such thing. I've a boat standing by to get rid of the bodies. You'll soon be floating in the sea, not known to history, only to surface once more as a playful pastiche eight hundred years from now.

CARADOC: Bitch! I see I'll have to do this myself. I'M A KILLER! I'M THE ANGEL OF DEATH! I KILL WHORES! I'm sure the

Barnwell Chronicler must have heard that. I believe he's quite understanding…

Freydis slashes Caradoc again with her blade.

CARADOC: Ah! That's torn it. Acta est fabula, plaudite!

Caradoc dies.

ERIK: What now?

FREYDIS: You must never breathe a word of this to anyone. Caradoc would revel in infamy in his watery grave if ever his fame grew. We must rid ourselves of the so-called Angel of Death once and for all, along with poor Roger. The boat is nearby. Drag the angel first.

Erik walks on stage carrying two babes, one in the crook of each arm. There is a windmill in the background.

ERIK: Hmm, smell that babes. That's good clean Swaffham air.

Mathilda walks on behind him, and takes one of the babies from him.

ERIK: Sorry Mathilda, I never did tell you that twins run in the family.

MATHILDA: Better late than never, I suppose. You did us proud in there.

ERIK: Well, now that I have all that midwifery knowledge, I was hardly going to stand outside twiddling my thumbs.

Freydis enters and coos at a baby.

FREYDIS: That was your best delivery yet. You know that they still ask after you in Cambridge? You could always put on your dress again.

ERIK: I think I've done with that. For the moment at least.

FREYDIS: I have a feeling that Erika and Erik will keep you busy for a while.

MATHILDA: Thank God that I now have such a domesticated husband. Aw! Erik's kissing Erika!

ERIK: That's right little one, you love your sister. But don't love her too much eh? You've got to let her be her own person.

FREYDIS: I'm sure my Erika is looking down and saying Amen to that!

ERIK: Oh, I don't know she'd say that. I'm sure she's had her fill of churchmen, clerks, scholars, and friars. Let's say "Awomen" instead!

FREYDIS: At least she'll be able to look down upon the two churches from this spot.

ERIK: And they won't be looking down on her for once! Aye, let's plant a memorial for Erika at the very top of the mill house, where she'll always hear the clapping of doves' wings.

FREYDIS AND MATHILDA: Awomen to that!

www.ingramcontent.com/pod-product-compliance
Lightning Source LLC
Chambersburg PA
CBHW020329130626
46549CB00003B/1088